my World of
Fabulous Fairies

Magic Meg

used to live in the Enchanted Forest
where she taught fledgling fairies,
pixies and elves to read runes and write
the magic alphabet. The most important
lessons she taught were how to fly
on moonbeams and gossamer into
the land of dreams.

Lucy Loveheart

has a special interest in fairies.
She is particularly fascinated by the
Enchanted Forest and spends much of
her time daydreaming about it.
She works mainly in watercolour,
collage, stickers and glitter, but she also
uses a little bit of magic and fairy dust.

We would like to dedicate this book to three wonderful fairy godmothers:
Joan, Connie and Mary.

This edition published in 2009 by
Zero to Ten Limited
Part of the Evans Publishing Group
2A Portman Mansions
Chiltern Street
London
W1U 6NR

First published in 2001 by Zero to Ten Limited.

Copyright © 2009 Zero to Ten Limited
Text © 2001 and 2009 Meg Clibbon
Illustrations © 2001 Lucy Clibbon

British Library Cataloguing in Publication Data
A catalogue record for this book
is available from the British Library

ISBN 978 1 84089 551 3

Printed in China on chlorine-free paper
from sustainably maintained forests.

Contents

What is a fairy?

*I*t is very difficult to describe
fairies because they are made out of
the imagination, not out of words.
Human beings very rarely meet fairies,
but those who have say that:
Fairies are usually smaller than humans.
Fairies are very secret.
Fairies live in an enchanted world.
Fairies do magic.

What do fairies look like?

There are lots of different kinds of fairies.

They come in many different shapes and sizes.

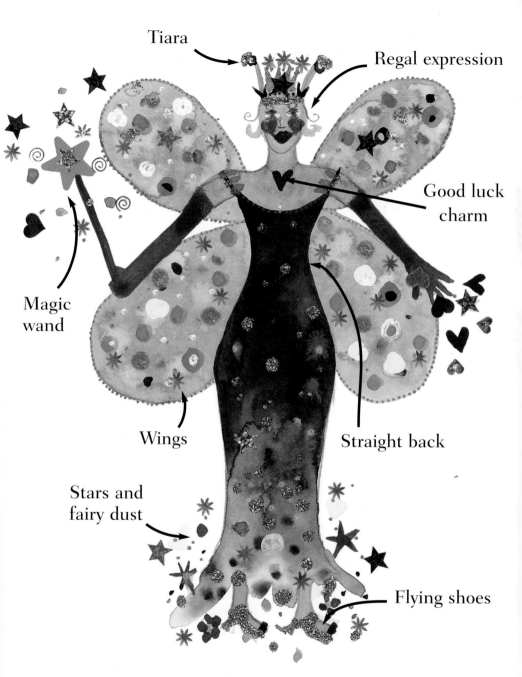

Tiara

Regal expression

Good luck charm

Magic wand

Wings

Straight back

Stars and fairy dust

Flying shoes

Whatever they look like, all fairies are very clever
and very magical.

Different types of fairies

Pixies: *very fast and lively*

Not all fairies are pretty, with gauzy, rainbow wings and frilly frocks. Some are rough and tough and very naughty. Others are spiteful and ugly.

Imps: *very naughty*

Goblins: *ugly little demons but clever*

Elves: *mischievous, but good leaders*

Sprites: *almost invisible*

Boggarts and Bugganes: *bad tempered*

Gnomes: *live underground*

Banshees: *female and scream a lot*

Leprechauns

They live in Ireland and look like very small old men. They like drinking a drink called poteen, which makes them rather spiteful. They guard treasure buried in pots and hide it at the end of rainbows. They carry two purses, one with a magic coin and one with fool's gold.

Will o' the wisps
(Jack-muh-lantern in the U.S.A.)
They live in swamps and marshes and lure humans into them with elf-fire.

The little people
They live in the Isle of Man, where people have always believed in fairies. They wear red caps and green jackets and hunt with multi-coloured hounds.

11

Where do fairies live?

Nobody is quite sure where
fairies live. They could live in dark
creepy caves or pretty little cottages,
under delicate dusky toadstools, or in
silvery cobweb nets swinging in the branches
of trees… but nobody really knows.
They appear magically at the most unexpected
moments and then they disappear again.

Where do they come from?
Where do they go to?
Where do you think
they live?

Fairy equipment

Fairies need special equipment and accessories
to help them with their work.

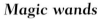

Magic wands

Flying shoes

**Cloak of
invisibility**

Book of spells

Magic potion

Flower fairy pollen

Fairy dust

Wings

Tiaras

Fairy words

gossamer

moonbeam

invisible

magic

wand

mischief

toadstool

secrets

Although fairies are very good at making spells, they are not very good at 'speling'. Can you help them match these pairs of singulars and plurals?

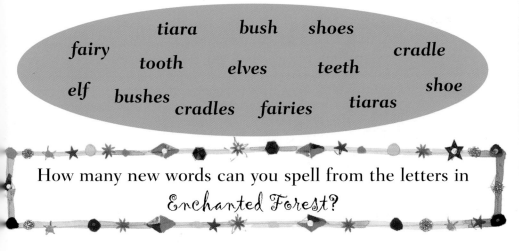

tiara   bush   shoes

fairy   cradle

tooth   elves   teeth

elf   bushes   shoe

cradles   fairies   tiaras

How many new words can you spell from the letters in *Enchanted Forest*?

Magic and spells

Fairies can do lots of magical things, like flying and making dreams come true. To do magic, it is essential to have a wand, some wings, some fairy dust, a tiara and a book of spells. A fairy's book of spells is very special and very secret, but here are some examples of typical fairy spells.

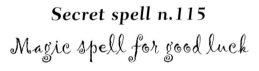

Secret spell n.115
Magic spell for good luck

You will need:

1 cup of daisy heads
2 spoonfuls of rosebuds
8 spoonfuls of morning dew
1 four-leafed clover
1 magic wand
1 mixing bowl

Directions

1. Mix the daisy heads, rosebuds and morning dew in mixing bowl.

2. Hold clover in your right hand.

3. Hold wand upright in left hand.

4. Close eyes and say, "Make my dream come true!"

Things that go wrong

Magic is a tricky thing and inexperienced fairies often get it wrong. It has been known for fairies to crash land in bramble bushes because they have not taken enough care of their wings. Fairy dust can have a nasty habit of making you sneeze. Even worse is when a magic spell makes a nightmare come true instead of a lovely dream. Not all fairies are good. Some are rather bad and they make things go wrong on purpose.

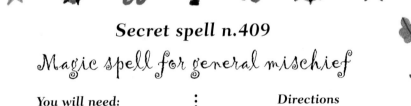

Secret spell n.409
Magic spell for general mischief

You will need:
1 cup of water
3 old conkers (or acorns)
1 handful of playground dust
1 spoonful of earth
4 old oak leaves

Directions
Place all the ingredients into an old tin at dead of night (around 9 o'clock). Hold wand in your right hand. Shout, "Banshee! Banshee!" and spell will be effective.

Fairy godmothers

These are special fairies because they come in human form. A fairy godmother can be young, but the favourite sort of fairy godmother is quite old, with a wrinkly face and a lovely smile.

Fairy godmothers are invited to lots of their godchildren's birthday parties. Parents expect special presents for their children, such as health, kindness, patience, obedience and good fortune... but the children would rather have toys or chocolate.

At the moment there are not many fairy godfathers, but this is considered to be very unfair and the Fairy Union (F.U.N.) is looking into it.

The Fairy Union (F.U.N)

The Fairy Union (F.U.N) insists that all fairies follow a strict code of conduct and obey the rules for fairies.

Rules

1. Always carry your wand, although it may be disguised as something else in certain circumstances.

2. Always be on the lookout for wicked witches who may cast horrid spells.

3. Look after your wings properly. Hang them up before you go to bed at night and polish them with fairy dust once a week.

4. Never stick out your tongue at a fairy godmother or the fairy king or you may get turned into a pumpkin.

Motto: Imagine magic and make believe

The Enchanted Forest

1. Gossamer clouds – *dreams come true when you sleep in these.*

2. Tooth fairy factory – *tooth fairies collect children's baby teeth when they fall out and grind them down to use in fairy dust.*

3. Stars – *used in dreams and for making glitter.*

4. Flying school – *all young fairies must attend.*

5. Store cupboard – *safe storage for magic dust.*

6. Wing polishers – *a specially-trained team of elves to polish fairies' wings.*

7. Boutique – *where fairies buy designer outfits.*

8. Wand shop – *for new wands and repairs.*

9.. Fairy ring – *the fairies' dancing ground.*

10. Wishing well – *the water from this well is used in magic potions.*

11. Toadstools – *where fairies sit to think or have their homes.*

12. Cobweb cradles – *baby fairies never cry when they are rocked in these.*

13. Allotment – *the fairies' vegetable garden.*

Famous fairies

Tinkerbell

Tinkerbell is a pretty little fairy who lives in Never Never
Land. This is in the story of *Peter Pan* by J.M. Barrie.
She has great fun with Peter Pan and the Lost Boys,
until a girl called Wendy comes to live there too. Tinkerbell
is so jealous that she causes a great deal of mischief.
Thankfully everything turns out well in the end.

Titania, Oberon and Puck

These are famous fairies in a play called
A Midsummer Night's Dream by William Shakespeare.
Titania is the very beautiful Queen of the Fairies
and Oberon is the powerful King of the Fairies. All through
the play they weave magic spells with the help of
their cunning little fairy servant, called Puck, who
makes life very difficult for a lot of people.

Famous fairy godmothers

The most famous fairy
godmothers appear in the stories of
Cinderella and *The Sleeping Beauty*.
In both stories the beautiful heroines need
a lot of help from their fairy godmothers.
Cinderella needs a coach, a new pair of glass slippers,
a handsome prince, a designer ball gown and
goodness knows what else. She is saved from
a life of housework by her very kind godmother.

Sleeping Beauty is imprisoned inside a castle
and would still be there if her fairy godmother
had not arranged for a passing prince to rescue
her and wake her up with a kiss. This must
have been rather a shock for her.

Fairy things to do

Make some fairy dust

Fairy dust helps you to
do magic properly.
Make your own fairy dust
by mixing together:
1 pinch of silver glitter
1 pinch of gold glitter
1 pinch of small sequins
Put together in a little bottle
marked fairy dust. Use sparingly
and sprinkle whenever needed.

Make a crown

Cut a strip of silver paper big
enough to wrap around your head.
Glue the ends together and decorate.

Make a wand

Wands are very good for helping spells to work.
To make your own, cut out a large star shape
and decorate with glitter, stars and hearts.
Attach this to a long stick.

Fairy bars

You will need:
75g butter
75g breakfast cereal (flakes or crispy rice)
1 tablespoon syrup
2 large chocolate bars
Fresh flowers to decorate

Directions
Asking an adult to help you, place butter into saucepan.
Add chocolate bars and syrup.
Melt on low heat. Turn off heat and stir in cereal
until coated. Put onto greased tray, and when almost
cool cut into bars. Arrange bars onto plate
and decorate with flower petals.

Practise flying

You'll need wings first. Make your wings by
cutting a piece of net into wing shapes.
Ask your fairy godmother to help you. Then
decorate with stars, heart shapes and glitter.
If you run or skip around the garden and
flap your arms up and down with wings
attached it almost feels like flying!

Daisybell's Fairy Challenge
the story of a fabulous fairy

One morning, Fairy Daisybell woke up in her mossy bed to find herself covered all over in soft silky rose petals.

"No wonder I felt so warm and snug," she thought. She jumped out of her bed, which was in an old bird's nest, and looked around.

The sun was slanting in long golden beams through the branches of the trees, the flowers were waking up and it was a beautiful morning in the Enchanted Forest. Just then, Fairy Daisybell noticed more of the rose petals stretching away from her, winding into the distance.

"I'll just get ready and then I'll follow that petal path and see where it leads," she said. So she washed her hands and face in a dewdrop and brushed her hair with a teasle. Then she cleaned her teeth with dandelion milk and, finally, polished her delicate gauzy wings.

"Now, let's see where this path leads," said Fairy Daisybell and she set off, munching her breakfast of honey seed toast on the way.

Just around the very first corner, she came across a little harvest mouse with big wet tears splashing off the end of his nose.

"Why, whatever is the matter?" cried Fairy Daisybell.

"My brothers and sisters ate all the breakfast and I'm hungry," wailed the little mouse. Fairy Daisybell looked at him. He had long glossy whiskers and a fat little tummy that looked as though it had quite a lot of breakfast in it already, but she was a kind little fairy so she gave him the rest of her honey seed toast, which he gobbled up in no time. He dried his tears, winked his bright little eyes at Daisybell and disappeared into the bushes.

Fairy Daisybell continued to follow the petal path and, before long, she found herself in the little woody glade where old Mrs Thumbkin the pixie lived. It was a beautiful toadstool house and Fairy Daisybell longed for a home just like it. The garden was full of herbs, vegetables and sweet-smelling flowers and there was a little chimney sticking out of the roof. She was just about to walk past the house when she stopped.

"Mrs Thumbkin usually waves to me from her window," she thought. "I wonder why there's no smoke coming from her chimney?"

She hurried up the path and peeped in through the door. Mrs Thumbkin was lying in her bed with the covers pulled up to her chin. The room was very cold.

"I think I've got the fairy flu," sniffed the old pixie. In no time at all Fairy Daisybell had made her a hot drink, lit the fire, plumped up her pillows and made her some breakfast.

"I'll get Dr Wiseowl to come and see you," she promised, "not to mention the pixie handyman because it's high time you had solar heating in this toadstool!"

And then she set off again.

At the next corner she met Fledge the squirrel, who was digging with his sharp little claws.

"Who on earth has dropped all these petals here?" he said. "I can't find any of my nuts."

"You've got hundreds of hiding places for your nuts," said Daisybell. "Why do you need to dig on this path?"

"I've lost a very special walnut, which I spent hours carving with my teeth as a present for someone. I think it's near here."

"Let's think hard," said Fairy Daisybell. "If it's so special you would have hidden it in a very special hiding place, so where would that be? A tree root? A rabbit hole? A..."

"Stop!" cried Fledge. "I've got it. I hid it in the walnut tree."

"Of course," laughed Fairy Daisybell.

"Thank you, thank you," said Fledge, and he scampered off into the trees.

Daisybell followed the petal path until, suddenly, at the edge of the Enchanted Forest it stopped. Fairy Daisybell gasped. There, in front of her, was the Fairy Queen's Palace, shimmering in the sunlight. Not only that, but there was the Fairy Queen herself, looking as beautiful as ever.

"Well, Fairy Daisybell, you are here at last. I've been waiting. It was I who laid that path for you to follow, but I expected you much sooner than this."

"Oh, Your Majesty," said Fairy Daisybell. "I'm so sorry. I was delayed on the way. Please forgive me."

"Fairy Daisybell, I know why you were delayed. You were being kind, thoughtful and clever to help others. And now you are being modest. These are all excellent qualities in a fairy and you have passed my Fairy Challenge with flying colours! As a result, I will grant you a wish. What shall it be?"

"I have everything I need except a house of my own," said Fairy Daisybell.

"Your wish is granted. You will have a toadstool house just like Mrs Thumbkin's – and I will even give it solar heating!" said the Fairy Queen. "Now come up to the Palace because I want to borrow your recipe for honey seed toast and, by the way, I have the most beautifully carved walnut to show you."